This book belongs to:

....

....

....

Retold by Gaby Goldsack
Illustrated by Kim Blundell (John Martin & Artists)
Designed by Jester Designs

Language consultant: Betty Root

ISBN 1-40545-556-X

This is a Parragon Publishing Book
This edition published in 2005

Parragon Publishing
Queen Street House
4 Queen Street
Bath BA1 1HE, UK

Copyright © Parragon 2002

Printed in India

Chicken Little

Helping Your Child Read

Learning to read is an exciting challenge for most children. From a very early age, sharing storybooks with children, talking about the pictures, and guessing what might happen next are all very important parts of the reading experience.

Sharing Reading

Set aside a regular quiet time to share reading with younger children, or to be available to encourage older children as they develop into independent readers.

First Readers are intended to encourage and support the early stages of learning to read. They present well-loved tales that children will enjoy hearing again and again. Familiarity helps children identify some of the words and phrases.

When you feel your child is ready to move ahead, encourage him or her to join in so that you read the story aloud together. Always pause to talk about the pictures. The easy-to-read speech bubbles in **First Readers** provide an excellent 'joining-in' activity. The bright, clear illustrations and matching text will help children understand the story.

Building Confidence

In time, children will want to read *to* you. When this happens, be patient and give continual praise. They may not read all the words correctly, but children's substitutions are often very good guesses.

The repetition in each book is especially helpful for building confidence. If your child cannot read a particular word, go back to the beginning of the sentence and read it together so the meaning is not lost. Most important, do not continue if your child is tired or just needs a break.

Reading alone

The next step is to ask your child to read alone. Try to be on hand to give help and support. Remember to give lots of encouragement and praise.

Along with other simple stories, **First Readers** will ensure that children will find reading an enjoyable and rewarding experience.

One day Chicken Little was in the field when an acorn fell on her head.

"Oh dear!" said Chicken Little. "The sky is falling. I must tell the king."

So Chicken Little
went off to tell the
king. On the way, she
met Cocky-Locky.

"Where are you going in such a hurry?"
asked Cocky-Locky.

What's the hurry?

10

"The sky is falling," said Chicken Little. "I'm going to tell the king."

"I'm coming with you," said Cocky-Locky.

On the way, Chicken Little and Cocky-Locky met Ducky-Lucky.

"Where are you going in such a hurry?" asked Ducky-Lucky.

"The sky is falling," said Chicken Little. "We are going to tell the king."

"I'm coming with you," said Ducky-Lucky.

On the way, Chicken Little, Cocky-Locky, and Ducky-Lucky met Goosey-Loosey.

"Where are you going in such a hurry?" asked Goosey-Loosey.

"The sky is falling," said Chicken Little. "We are going to tell the king."

"I'm coming with you," said Goosey-Loosey.

They all walked on until they met
Foxy-Loxy.

"Where are you going in such a hurry?" asked Foxy-Loxy.

"The sky is falling," said Chicken Little. "We are going to tell the king."

The sky is falling!

We must see the king.

"Ah," smiled Foxy-Loxy, who was a sly young fox. "You are going the wrong way. Follow me. I will show you the way."

So Chicken Little, Cocky-Locky, Ducky-Lucky, and Goosey-Loosey followed Foxy-Loxy.

Is this the way?

They walked on and on. At last they came to a cave. "Follow me," said Foxy-Loxy. "This is a shortcut."

19

But the cave was really
Foxy-Loxy's den.
She smiled as Cocky-Locky,
Ducky-Lucky, and
Goosey-Loosey followed her.

Chicken Little was about to follow when Cocky-Locky cried out loud, "Cock-a-doodle-doo!"

Chicken Little knew that
something was wrong.

She turned and ran away.
She ran and ran.

22

Chicken Little did not stop until she got to the barnyard. Then she looked around for her friends.

Chicken Little waited and waited, but her friends did not come back.

Chicken Little knew she was a
very lucky hen.

Chicken Little never did tell the king that the sky was falling. But the sky never was falling, was it?

Chicken Little was a very silly hen!

But she never went near a fox again.

Read and Say

How many of these words can you say? The pictures will help you. Look back in your book and see if you can find the words in the story.

acorn

cave

Chicken Little

Cocky-Locky

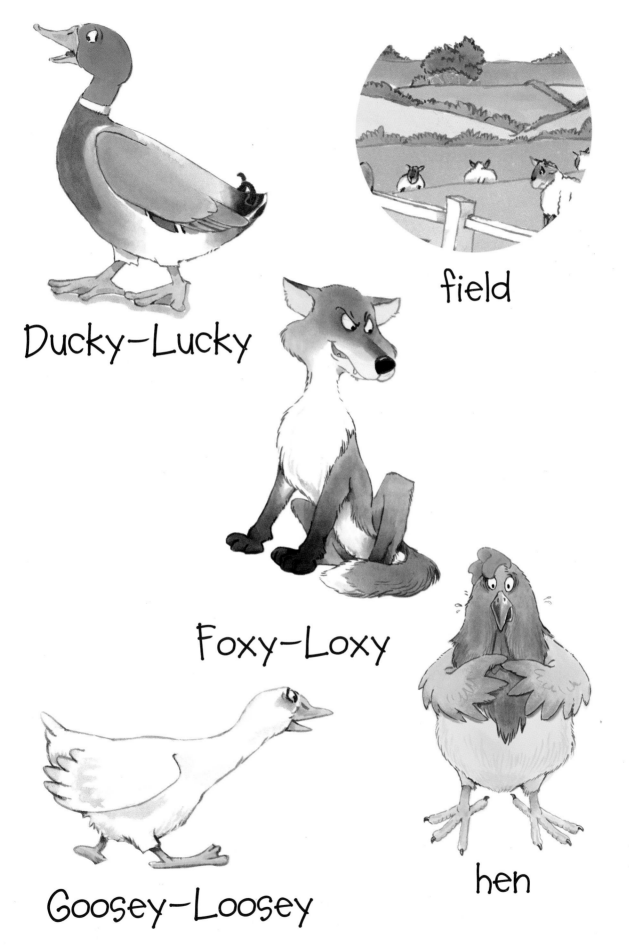

Ducky-Lucky

field

Foxy-Loxy

hen

Goosey-Loosey

29